SCARY TALES RETOLD™

HANSEL AND GRETEL AND THE HAUNTED HUT

by Wiley Blevins • illustrated by Steve Cox

RED CHAIR
•PRESS•

Please visit our website at **www.redchairpress.com** for more high-quality products for young readers.

About the Author

Wiley Blevins has taught elementary school in both the United States and South America. He has also written over 70 books for children and 15 for teachers, as well as created reading programs for schools in the U.S. and Asia with Scholastic, Macmillan/McGraw-Hill, Houghton-Mifflin Harcourt, and other publishers. Wiley currently lives and writes in New York City.

About the Artist

Steve Cox lives in London, England. He first designed toys and packaging for other people's characters. But he decided to create his own characters and turned full time to illustrating. When he is not drawing books he plays lead guitar in a rock band.

Publisher's Cataloging-In-Publication Data

Blevins, Wiley.
  Hansel and Gretel and the haunted hut / by Wiley Blevins ; illustrated by Steve Cox.

  pages : illustrations ; cm. -- (Scary tales retold)

  Summary: "Poor Hansel and Gretel, cast out on their own by a wicked stepmother. The brother and sister set off into the woods and discover a candy cottage, only to be tricked by the ravens and evil witch inside. When Gretel saves her brother, it looks like the witch is gone for good, but is she?"--Provided by publisher.
  Issued also as an ebook.
  ISBN: 978-1-63440-096-1 (library hardcover)
  ISBN: 978-1-63440-097-8 (paperback)

  1. Brothers and sisters--Juvenile fiction. 2. Witches--Juvenile fiction. 3. Brothers and sisters--Fiction. 4. Witches--Fiction. 5. Fairy tales. 6. Horror tales. I. Cox, Steve, 1961- II. Title. III. Title: Based on (work) Hansel and Gretel.

PZ7.B618652 Ha 2016
[E]   2015940013

Scary Tales Retold first published by:
Red Chair Press LLC   PO Box 333   South Egremont, MA 01258-0333

Printed in the United States of America
Distributed in the U.S. by Lerner Publisher Services. www.lernerbooks.com

0516 1 CBGF16

Once upon a time, there lived a brother and sister named Hansel and Gretel. They lived in a small, stone house with their father and stepmother. Their stepmother had no love for them.

"Take those children into the forest," said the stepmother to their father. "And make sure they never come back."

So, Hansel's and Gretel's father loaded them into a cart. And took them deep into the forest.

After many hours, they stopped by a stream. "Go and get sticks for a fire," said their father. "I will stay with the cart."

So, Hansel and Gretel walked farther into the forest. Six black birds began to follow them.

In time, Hansel and Gretel returned with the sticks. But their father was nowhere to be found.

"How will we get home?" asked Gretel. She began to cry.

"Stepmother asked father to leave us here," said Hansel. He pointed to a path he had made from breadcrumbs. "But this path will show us the way home."

Hansel and Gretel began following
the crumbs. With each step, the
forest grew darker and darker.
Then suddenly, the crumb path ended.

Hansel and Gretel looked around.
They saw eyes glowing in the dark.
Eyes high. Eyes low.
Eyes peeking behind trees.
And eyes moving toward them.
But no crumbs.

"Where are the crumbs?" asked Hansel.
"We have to get out of here."

"Look. The birds are making a
new path with them," said Gretel.
"They must know a faster way home."

"Come! Come!" screeched the birds.

"Hurry!" said Hansel. "Follow them."

"I see a light in that hut by the lake,"
said Gretel. "The birds must
be taking us there."

Hansel and Gretel ran to the hut.
"Go in! Go in!" screeched the birds.

Hansel and Gretel went up to the hut's door.

"It smells like candy," said Gretel.

A small piece broke off. Hansel took a bite. "It tastes like candy, too. Can it be?"

Just then the door creaked open. An old woman looked out at them. "Come in my sweets," she said. "You must be starving."

And as Hansel and Gretel went inside, the six black birds laughed.

Hansel and Gretel couldn't believe what they saw in the hut. Bowls of their favorite foods filled a long table.

A big cooking pot boiled beside a large metal cage.

"What's the cage for?" asked Gretel.

"My birds," said the old woman. The six black birds flew in. They circled above Hansel and Gretel. The flapping of their wings sent an icy chill up Hansel and Gretel's backs.

The old woman pointed her bony, crooked finger at Hansel. "Put this bowl of water in the cage," she said. "My birds need water before they eat their *special* meal."

And as soon as Hansel went inside the cage,
the old woman locked the door.

"What are you doing?" cried Hansel.

"I am going to fatten you up," said
the old woman. "Then I am going
to cook you. And feed you to my birds."

"No!" yelled Gretel. She pushed the old woman away. The old woman fell backwards and into the boiling pot. Quickly Gretel slammed the lid shut.

Then Gretal unlocked the cage.

At that moment, the hut's door burst open.
There stood a tall, angry hunter.

"Why are you in my house?" he yelled.

"Your house?" said Hansel. "The old woman with the birds lives here."

"That's impossible," said the hunter. "That old woman died a year ago."

Just then the cooking pot lid rattled.

The old woman popped out of the pot.
Her ghostly laugh filled the hut.

"Get out of here," yelled the hunter. "Now!"
And he dashed into the forest.

But as Hansel and Gretel ran for the door . . .

It slammed shut and locked.

"You will never leave this hut,
my sweets," said the old woman.

And Hansel and Gretel were never seen in the forest again.

THE END